THERE W[illegible] OLD LADY WHO SWALLOWED SOME BOOKS!

by Lucille Colandro
Illustrated by Jared Lee

CARTWHEEL BOOKS
An Imprint of Scholastic Inc.

For Karen, Betsy, and Cecelia
—the best school pals
a gal could have.
—L.C.

To Jeannie Phillips
—J.L.

ISBN 978-0-545-49108-2

12 11 10 9 8 7 6 5 4 3 2 1 12 13 14 15 16 17/0

Printed in the U.S.A. 40

This edition first printing, September 2012

There was an old lady who swallowed some books.
I don't know why she swallowed those books,
but she didn't get any looks.

There was an old lady who swallowed a pen.
She was happy again when she swallowed that pen.

She swallowed the pen to write in the books.
I don't know why she swallowed the books,
but she didn't get any looks.

There was an old lady who swallowed a pencil case.
Without leaving a trace, she swallowed that pencil case.

She swallowed the pencil case to hold the pen.
She swallowed the pen to write in the books.

I don't know why she swallowed the books,
but she didn't get any looks.

There was an old lady who swallowed a ruler.

She couldn't look cooler swallowing that ruler.

She swallowed the ruler to measure the pencil case.
She swallowed the pencil case to hold the pen.
She swallowed the pen to write in the books.

I don't know why she swallowed the books,
but she didn't get any looks.

There was an old lady who swallowed a folder.

She didn't feel any older when she swallowed the folder.

She swallowed the folder to protect the ruler.
She swallowed the ruler to measure the pencil case.
She swallowed the pencil case to hold the pen.

She swallowed the pen to write in the books.
I don't know why she swallowed the books,
but she didn't get any looks.

There was an old lady who swallowed some chalk.
She didn't balk when she swallowed that chalk.

She swallowed the chalk to decorate the folder.

She swallowed the folder to protect the ruler.

She swallowed the ruler to measure the pencil case.

She swallowed the pencil case to hold the pen.

She swallowed the pen to write in the books.

I don't know why she swallowed the books,
but she didn't get any looks.

There was an old lady who swallowed a bag.

She didn't brag when she swallowed that bag.

The old lady didn't fuss when around the corner came a big yellow school bus.

She started a cheer that she could not hold back
and out popped her brand-new backpack.

Have a great school year!